Miami Heat

John Nichols

Published by Creative Education
123 South Broad Street, Mankato, Minnesota 56001
Creative Education is an imprint of The Creative Company

Designed by Rita Marshall

Photos by: Allsport Photography, Associated Press/Wide World Photos,
Focus on Sports, NBA Photos, UPI/Corbis-Bettmann, and SportsChrome.

Photo page 1: Bimbo Coles
Photo title page: Billy Owens

Library of Congress Cataloging-in-Publication Data

Nichols, John.
Miami Heat / John Nichols.
p. cm. — (NBA today)
Summary: Describes the background and history of the Miami Heat pro
basketball team.
ISBN 0-88682-879-1

1. Miami Heat (Basketball team)—History—Juvenile literature.
[1. Miami Heat (Basketball team)—History. 2. Basketball—History.]
I. Title. II. Series: NBA today (Mankato, Minn.)

GV885.52.M53R36 1997   96-6529
796.323'64'09759381—dc21

First edition

5 4 3 2 1

Miami, Florida, has long been one of America's tourism hot spots. The warm sun, endless beaches, and numerous attractions provide a playground for vacationers young and old. Located on the southeastern coast of Florida, Miami is a melting pot of cultures. People from around the country and around the world have flocked there to enjoy the tropical climate.

In Miami, sports and leisure are not just hobbies—they are a way of life and a top industry of the city. Some of the city's biggest attractions are its professional sports teams. The Miami Dolphins of the National Football League have

Star rebounder Billy Owens.

delighted packed stadiums, winning two championships since 1967. The National Hockey League and Major League Baseball established franchises in Miami in the early 1990s, with the addition of hockey's Florida Panthers and baseball's Florida Marlins.

Indeed, the city of Miami has a rich sports menu to choose from, but perhaps the hottest ticket in town belongs to the National Basketball Association's (NBA) Miami Heat. Established as an expansion franchise in 1988, the Heat have slowly but surely become a winner in South Florida. With champion coach Pat Riley and superstar players Alonzo Mourning and Tim Hardaway, Miami has turned up the heat on the rest of the NBA, and the temperature won't drop until a championship banner hangs in the Miami Arena.

In August, builders broke ground on Miami Arena, the Heat's new home.

THE HEAT RISES IN SOUTH FLORIDA

The drive to bring NBA basketball to Miami began in May of 1986, when three men from vastly different backgrounds announced their plans to attract an expansion team to South Florida. Former Philadelphia 76ers All-Star player and coach Billy Cunningham, Broadway producer Zev Buffman, and shipping magnate Ted Arison formed an unlikely alliance in the effort to bring the NBA to Miami. However different their backgrounds might have been, they each saw the potential chemistry between the NBA and Miami's sports-crazy fans.

"I've played in this league, and I've coached in this league," said an enthusiastic Cunningham. "I've been around enough cities to know Miami will be a great NBA town."

Rony Seikaly, a powerhouse at center.

Buffman and Arison provided the partnership's financial muscle, while Cunningham brought decades of basketball experience. It was a combination that couldn't be beat. In April of 1987, the NBA announced that the Miami Heat would be one of the league's four new teams. The Heat and their expansion partner, the Charlotte Hornets, would begin play in 1988, while the two other new teams—Minnesota and Orlando—would wait until 1989.

That didn't leave much time to build an entire organization. But for Cunningham and his partners, the challenge of building something from scratch was part of the excitement. Cunningham knew that his expansion team would not have a lot of talent, especially on offense. It would be important to hire a coach who was a defensive-minded teacher, who could squeeze every ounce of talent out of his players. With those qualifications in mind, Cunningham hired Detroit Pistons assistant coach Ron Rothstein as Miami's first head coach. Rothstein had been widely credited for being the mastermind behind the Pistons' bruising defensive schemes, which helped make Detroit one of the league's best teams. "Ron's a fine young coach," said Pistons head man Chuck Daly. "I think he's the ideal guy for a young team. He loves to teach the game."

Rothstein and Cunningham agreed to build the team with young players who had a future, not past-their-prime NBA veterans. They wouldn't give in to the "win now" pressures that had led young teams of the past into disastrous decisions. Rothstein was fond of saying: "Shortcuts lead down the road to failure." So the Heat would take no shortcuts. Cunningham and Rothstein decided that they would play it smart—the Heat would be built through the draft. "If the wins didn't come right away," said Rothstein, "that's okay. It only means they'll come in bigger numbers later on."

HEAT FILL CENTER WITH SEIKALY

1 9 8 8

The fiercely determined Ron Rothstein was named the Heat's first head coach.

When the Heat chose Syracuse University center Rony Seikaly with their first pick in the 1988 draft, they knew he wasn't polished. "Rony had some rough edges coming out of college, no doubt," observed Rothstein. "We knew we'd probably get more production the first year from the guys we took later in the draft, but Seikaly's such a good athlete, we knew if we hung in there and let him learn, he'd be a good one."

Rothstein was right. Both shooting guard Kevin Edwards of DePaul and rugged power forward Grant Long of Eastern Michigan had more productive rookie seasons than Seikaly. But the Heat were convinced that the big center had a world of potential. The 7-foot, 250-pound Seikaly was born in Lebanon and grew up in Greece. He didn't watch much basketball as a youngster, and he didn't start playing the game until after his junior year in high school. Even then, only his impressive size and strong running ability got him any notice from American colleges. After enrolling at national power Syracuse, Seikaly managed to make the team even though he didn't have a lot to offer right away. Head coach Jim Boeheim recognized the youngster's intelligence and raw ability. "Rony is the only center I've ever had who can call for the ball in three languages," joked Boeheim. "Rony put his mind

9

Early Miami stars Willie Burton . . .

. . . and guard Steve Smith.

to learning this game, and the kid's a great athlete. I learned early never to doubt him."

By the time Seikaly completed his career at Syracuse, his hard work had made him one of the nation's top talents. When he was selected by the Heat, he was put in a situation in which he would get the floor time necessary to develop his skills. But being the number one draft pick would also carry some unwanted weight. Seikaly, ready or not, was the "franchise" in Miami.

1 · 9 · 8 · 8

Rory Sparrow sank Miami's first field goal one minute into the first game on November 5.

When the team started off its first season by losing 17 straight games and setting an NBA record for futility, much of the media attention focused on the struggles of the young center. Being the most visible player on a team that posted a record of 15–67 in 1988–89 was not easy, but to his credit, Seikaly used the negatives to motivate himself. "All of us learned that first year what it took to be a professional," said a confident Seikaly. "They say what doesn't kill you makes you stronger, and Grant, Kevin, and I all got a lot stronger that season."

RICE AND DOUGLAS BOLSTER HEAT

In their second season, the Heat did not waver from their plan to build a winner through the college draft. With the fourth pick in the first round in 1989, the Heat chose University of Michigan forward Glen Rice. The 6-foot-8 Rice had carried the Wolverines to a national championship in 1989, averaging 30 points a contest during the tournament. His biggest weapon was a deadly long-range jump shot, but he also had an explosive first step and leaping ability that al-

12

lowed him to drive for easy baskets. For a team that needed scoring help, Glen Rice was the definite answer.

"We think Glen has the potential to be a great scorer in this league," said Rothstein of his new talent. "He'll need to work on his defense and his conditioning, but that will come. He's just a baby right now."

In reality, Rothstein had an entire roster of "babies." Three of the five starters had only one year of experience; the two others, Rice and second-round pick Sherman Douglas, were rookies. The selection of Douglas gave Miami its first real point guard. His uncanny passing ability and unusual composure for a rookie helped jump-start a Miami offense that had been among the league's worst in 1988. More importantly, Douglas had been Seikaly's teammate at Syracuse, and the chemistry between the two was obvious.

1 9 8 9

Kevin Edwards, the team's number two draft pick, became the team's number one scorer.

"It's great that I could team up with Rony again," smiled Douglas. "He's had it tough so far, but I'm going to get him the ball, and he knows it. We make a good combination."

The additions of Douglas and the sure-shooting Rice made life easier on the inside for Seikaly, and his production increased dramatically. His season averages of 16.6 points and 10.4 rebounds opened a lot of eyes around the league, and Seikaly was named the NBA's Most Improved Player for 1989. Douglas earned honors, too, making the NBA All-Rookie first team by scoring 14.3 points a game and dishing out 7.6 assists.

The Heat, however, didn't see much improvement in the win column. The young team still tended to self-destruct in close games, and following an 18-win season in 1989, the Heat improved only marginally to 24–58 in 1990. Cunning-

Sherman Douglas was the first Heat player to score 1,000 points and make 500 assists.

ham had expected to see more improvement in his young team by the end of the third year, and now it appeared to him that the franchise was stagnating. The Heat had chosen to build with young players, but many experts around the league thought that the team had "thrown the kids to the wolves." By that, they meant that too much was expected from players who were not experienced enough to produce. Cunningham still believed his team had strong talent, but he knew a move needed to be made. Ron Rothstein resigned at the end of the 1990–91 season, and Cunningham made the decision to hire an experienced head coach—a leader who could mold the Heat's young talent into a cohesive, consistent winner.

LOUGHERY, SMITH BRING BETTER DAYS

When fiery Kevin Loughery took over as the new head coach of the Heat, many of his players were surprised to find out that he had been around the NBA—as a coach or a player—longer than many of them had been alive. Loughery had held down a job in pro basketball since 1962, and he possessed a wealth of experience. His coaching career began in 1972, when he took over as player/coach for the Philadelphia 76ers for the final 31 games. The next year he moved on to the American Basketball Association (ABA) and won two championships with the acrobatic Julius "Dr. J" Erving and the New York Nets before moving on. Loughery had stints with three more teams before retiring and going into broadcasting in 1988. But when

"Iron Man" Grant Long.

High-scoring forward Glen Rice.

Cunningham—his old friend from the 76ers—came calling, saying he needed a coach, Loughery came out of retirement.

"I think the Heat have put together a great bunch of talented kids, but talent isn't everything," said Loughery. "I've got to instill a winning spirit in these guys. Some nights things don't go right, and that's where attitude takes over. I'm here for my attitude."

Along with Loughery's feisty attitude, the Heat would also add a new weapon to their arsenal. With their first-round pick in the 1991 draft, the team took Michigan State guard Steve Smith. The 6-foot-8 Smith reminded a lot of people of another guy who played at Michigan State and did pretty well—Earvin "Magic" Johnson. Their similarities went deeper than just being from the same school. Both had the unique combination of size and ball-handling skill that made them capable of doing things not often seen from players their height. They could play the big-man's game by rebounding and scoring from the post, or play the small-man's game with long-range shooting and pinpoint passing. Smith brought a big package of talent to the Heat, and with all the comparisons to Johnson, a heavy burden of expectations.

Bimbo Coles tied Grant Long's Heat record for the most games played in a rookie season (82).

But the quiet Smith didn't let the attention bother him. "It's an honor for people to compare me to Magic," said a humble Smith. "He's a guy I've admired since I was little. But I can't try to be the next Magic Johnson. I can only be the first Steve Smith."

The maturing Heat lineup had added yet another weapon. A Miami franchise that only three seasons before had looked like a "daycare," according to one opposing NBA coach, now seemed on the verge of finally becoming a winner. The young

Electrifying center Rony Seikaly (pages 18–19).

players who seemed lost early on—like Seikaly and Rice—were now giving lessons on the court instead of taking them. An early-season trade of Sherman Douglas (who was holding out in a contract dispute) to the Boston Celtics for 6-foot-6 point guard Brian Shaw also paid dividends by giving Miami one of the league's biggest and strongest backcourts.

The patience of the Heat's front office was finally rewarded, as the team battled to a 38–44 mark and qualified for the playoffs as the Eastern Conference's eighth seed. Miami was the first of the four late-1980s expansion teams to reach the post-season. The experience was brief, as the top-seeded Chicago Bulls, led by Michael Jordan, steamrolled the Heat in three straight games, but it was also satisfying. "We lost to a better team," explained Loughery. "But I'm very proud of what our guys accomplished."

After their playoff season of 1991, the Heat had high hopes for more progress the following year. But a knee injury to Smith kept him out of the lineup for 34 games, and by the time he returned, the team was out of contention and finished 36–46. With the bad taste of a lost season still fresh in their memory, Seikaly, Rice, and Smith all rededicated their efforts in 1993. "We're not kids anymore," proclaimed Rice. "Our fans have been patient with us. Now it's time to reward them with a big season."

The Heat did post their best season ever in 1993–94, going 42–40, once again making the playoffs. The talented threesome of Seikaly, Rice, and Smith carried the team through a strong regular season, but the post-season once again proved to be a disappointment. The Heat were eliminated by the Atlanta Hawks in the first round, three games to two. The promised "big season" had not materialized, and the winds of change began to blow through the team.

During the off-season and early into the 1994–95 campaign, the entire Heat organization went through a drastic upheaval. Seikaly, Smith, and Grant Long were traded away, while versatile Billy Owens and workhorse power forward Kevin Willis were brought in. The Arison family bought out Billy Cunningham's share of the team, and with the change in ownership came a change in coaches. Alvin Gentry was named to replace Kevin Loughery. With all the changes on the court and in the front office, the Heat suffered through a

Keith Askins dished out a career-high 16 rebounds in a game against Washington.

Scoring sensation Kevin Willis.

21

Early '90s standout Brian Shaw.

setback season in 1994–95, finishing 32–50. Rice said it best when he described the year as "an experiment gone bad." When Gentry was fired at the end of the season, many fans feared that the franchise was again in a downward spiral.

"RILES" ADDS CHAMPIONSHIP FLAVOR TO HEAT

1 9 9 5

Coach Pat Riley's players posted a 7-1 record at home for the first month of the season.

On September 2, 1995, Miami's beleaguered fans got a surprise. Pat Riley, architect of the championship Los Angeles Lakers teams of the 1980s, and more recently coach of the powerful New York Knicks, had taken the job of team president and head coach of the Heat. In Riley's 13-year coaching career, his teams had never failed to make the playoffs, and they had won four NBA championships. The Heat were hoping Riley's championship luster would rub off on their franchise, but Riley knew the team would need more than just his reputation. He had asked for total control over basketball decisions before taking the job, knowing that in order to implement his plan, he had to be able to do it "the Riley way."

"We're going to build this franchise into a winner the only way I know how," explained a serious Riley. "We're going to bring in the best players, and we'll work harder than anybody else. It's that simple."

Riley had always received a good deal of publicity for his stylish suits and movie-star looks, but in reality, the coach was a believer in substance over style. Skinned knees and sweaty uniforms were what Pat Riley really stood for, and hard work was always at the center of his coaching strategy. It was not uncommon for Riley to put his star-studded Lakers and Knicks

1 9 9 5

Billy Owens racked up 19 points, 10 rebounds, and 10 assists for his first triple-double.

teams through three-hour practices and intensive film study to help them keep their winning edge. "Coach Riley looks like a guy who just walked off a magazine cover," laughed former Lakers star Magic Johnson. "But really he's an old gym rat. He eats, drinks, and sleeps basketball."

One of Riley's coaching tactics was to build his team around a dominant center. He had structured the Lakers' championship teams around Hall of Famer Kareem Abdul-Jabbar and had taken the Knicks to the NBA finals on the broad shoulders of Patrick Ewing. "Everything in basketball is easier if you have a star big man," said Riley. "Scoring

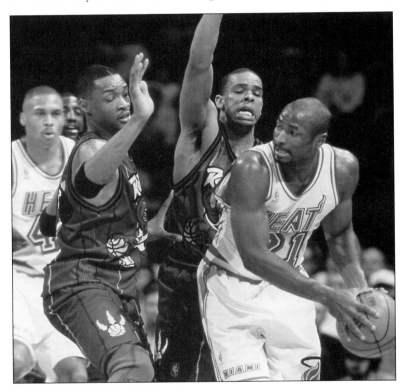

Voshon Lenard, a tenacious guard.

points is easier, defense is easier, coaching is much easier. That's why I want to build this team from the inside out."

With the trade of Seikaly the season before, the Heat did not have a dominant center on the roster. But Riley was not discouraged. On November 3, 1995—the night before the season opener—Riley arranged a trade that sent Glen Rice, center Matt Geiger, and former first-round pick Khalid Reeves to the Charlotte Hornets for guard Pete Myers, center LeRon Ellis, and All-Star center Alonzo Mourning. Riley had landed his dominant center, but he wasn't done yet. Now he needed a point guard to get the ball to Mourning. Within three months, Riley had made another deal, acquiring All-Star point man Tim Hardaway.

1 9 9 6

Tim Hardaway set a club record with 19 assists during a win over the Milwaukee Bucks.

The trades for Mourning and Hardaway immediately gave Miami a potent one-two punch offensively and defensively. Mourning's physical strength and fierce attitude had made him a defensive stalwart since his rookie year. But what many fans overlooked was that the former Georgetown University All-American had developed a dangerous and varied offensive attack. His 20-points-per-game average gave testimony to the fact that the big man could do it all.

Hardaway had established himself as one of the league's finest point guards while at Golden State. His devastating cross-over dribble and amazing speed had left hundreds of dazed defenders wondering why they had bothered to get out of bed. When opposing guards would back away to avoid getting beat on the drive, Hardaway would simply pull up and drain a three-pointer. "I think playing with Alonzo will be a great opportunity for me," said a smiling Hardaway.

All-Star veteran Dan Majerle (pages 26–27).

"Having him there down low makes it hard for teams to gang up on me. We'll definitely help each other."

On the defensive side, Hardaway's quickness allowed him to harass opposing ball handlers and prowl the passing lanes for errant passes. "With Tim and Zo [Mourning], I feel comfortable that we've got the foundation laid," said Riley. "There's a lot more work to be done, but it's a good start."

With their two new stars, the Heat bounced back to match their best-ever record of 42–40 in their first season under Riley and secured the eighth seed in the Eastern Conference playoffs. The Heat's reward? A first-round matchup against the team that had just completed the greatest regular season in the history of the league, the Chicago Bulls. The Bulls, with their 72–10 record, swept the Heat three straight in convincing style.

"No excuses. We got beat up," said a stoic Riley. "The Bulls are a championship team and we are not . . . yet."

1 9 9 6

Forward P.J. Brown tallied a career-high 30 points in a game with the Nets before joining the Miami Heat.

HEAT PLOT AN AGGRESSIVE FUTURE

With Pat Riley at the helm, Miami has made a commitment to winning a championship. For so many seasons, while the Heat pursued greatness, they consistently came up short. But, as Riley would say, "That was then and this is now."

The 1996–97 season indicated that the Heat have been heading in the right direction. The addition of All-Star shooting guard Dan Majerle through free agency allowed the Heat to team another weapon with the dynamic duo of Mourning and Hardaway. Riley will continue to build the Heat in his

Future Heat star Jamal Mashburn.

Double-digit scorer Tim Hardaway.

Miami's All-Star center Alonzo Mourning.   31

Miami newcomer Isaac Austin was voted the Most Improved Player in the NBA.

own image: They will be hard-working, intense, and obsessed with perfection. "I'm here to build a championship team," said Riley when he was hired. "Not a good team or a decent team, but a champion."

With his team leading the Atlantic Division, Riley pulled off another big trade midway through the season, sending three players—forwards Kurt Thomas and Martin Muursepp and guard Sasha Danilovic—to the Dallas Mavericks in exchange for Jamal Mashburn, who, when he was drafted with a lottery pick in 1993, was hailed as a key element in the Mavericks' quest for a championship. Mashburn gave the Heat a legitimate NBA star at the forward position and quickly meshed with the stars Riley already had at guard and center.

The Heat won the Atlantic Division and again found themselves in the playoffs. In the first round, they met a surprisingly scrappy Orlando Magic team led by Penny Hardaway. It took Voshon Lenard's 13 third-quarter points and Tim Hardaway's five points in the final five minutes of game five for the Heat to win the series and advance to the second round against Riley's former team, the Knicks. Down three games to one, the Heat battled back and forced the series to a game seven. Hardaway and Mourning combined for 60 points and a victory. The Heat once again faced Chicago, this time in the Eastern Conference Finals. Miami put up a valiant fight, but fell to the defending-champion Bulls.

Though the Heat ended the year short of their ultimate goal, with NBA Coach of the Year Pat Riley calling the shots, Miami fans can expect a championship Heat-wave to come their way again in the near future.